EVE TITUS

THE KITTEN WHO COULDN'T PURR

Pictures by
AMREI FECHNER

Morrow Junior Books / New York

Karen
put a big bowl of milk
on the floor
and called her kittens.

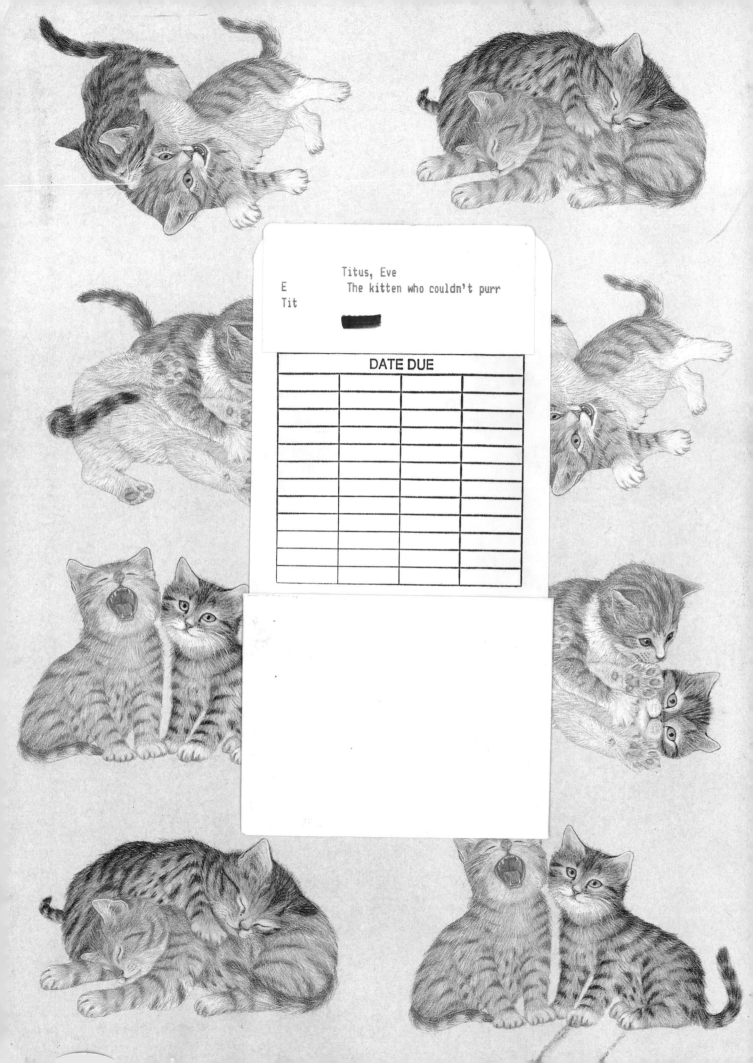

Titus, Eve

E   The kitten who couldn't purr
Tit

DATE DUE

Dedications

For my
young friends
Demitri and Nina
(and their puppy dog
Toto)
—E.T.

For my
children
Max and Julia
(and their kitten
Lola)
—A.F.

"Here, Jenny! Here, Judy!
Here, Jimmy! Here, Jonathan!"

The kittens all came running
and lapped up the milk very fast.

"Did you like the milk?" asked Karen.

"Purr," said Jenny.
"Purr, purr," said Judy.
"Purr, purr, purr," said Jimmy.
"Purr, purr, purr, purr, purr,"
said Jenny and Judy and Jimmy together.

Jonathan tried to purr, but he couldn't.

"If you liked the milk,
then why don't you purr?"
Karen asked Jonathan.
"Purring is like saying 'Thank you.'
Please purr, little kitten!"

Again he tried, but he couldn't.

He knew Karen couldn't tell
how hard he was trying,
for she said,
"Rude Jonathan!
If you won't purr,
then you're not polite.
Go outside!"

Jonathan went outside,
as sad as he could be.

I'm not at all rude,
he said to himself.
I'll learn how to purr
so I can say "Thank you."
If I go down the road,
maybe I'll meet someone
who'll show me how.

So he walked along
  and walked along
    and walked along
until he met
      a
        little
          red

H E N !

"Please, Hen, how do you purr?"

"Like this—CLUCK! CLUCK! CLUCK!"

"But that's not purring, it's clucking."

"Naturally! I'm a hen,
not a cat or a kitten."
    And away went the little red hen.

Jonathan still couldn't purr,
but did he stop trying? NO!
He walked along
        and walked along
            and walked along
until he met
            a
            large
                white

D U C K !
"Please, Duck, how do you purr?"

"Like this—QUACK! QUACK! QUACK!"

"But that's not purring, it's quacking."

"Naturally! I'm a duck, not a cat or a kitten."
And away went the large white duck.

Jonathan still couldn't purr,
but did he stop trying? NO!
He walked along
      and walked along
        and walked along
until he met
         a
           fat
             pink

P I G !

"Please, Pig, how do you purr?"

"Like this—OINK! OINK! OINK!"

"But that's not purring, it's oinking."

"Naturally! I'm a pig,
not a cat or a kitten."
        And away went the fat pink pig
        and her ten children.

Jonathan still couldn't purr,
but did he stop trying? NO!
He walked along
    and walked along
        and walked along
            until he met
                a
                    big
                        brown

C O W !

"Please, Cow, how do you purr?"

"Like this—MOO! MOO! MOO!"

"But that's not purring, it's mooing."

"Naturally! I'm a cow, not a cat or a kitten."
And away went the big brown cow.

Jonathan still couldn't purr,
but did he stop trying? NO!
He walked along and walked along
and walked along until he met

a

tall

gray

D O N K E Y !
"Please, Donkey, how do you purr?"

"Like this—HEE-HAW! HEE-HAW! HEE-HAW!"

"But that's not purring, it's hee-hawing."

"Naturally. I'm a donkey,
not a cat or a kitten."
And away went
the tall gray donkey.

Jonathan said sadly,
"I'll never learn to purr,
so I'll give up
and go home."

But just then,
along came
a
small
black

P U P P Y —
HIS FRIEND TOTO!
"I'm sad, Toto, because I can't purr."

"Don't be sad," said the puppy.
"There are other ways to say 'Thank you.'
My way is to wag my tail. Can you wag yours?
I'm your friend, so I'll help you. Watch me!"

WAGGITY-WAG went Toto's tail from side to side.
WAGGITY-WAG, fast, faster, FASTEST!

Slow as a snail went Jonathan's tail at first,
up and down, round and round, the *wrong* way.
But he waggity-wagged, over and over and over,
until his tail went side to side, the *right* way!

"Am I a good tail-wagger?" asked Jonathan.

"I'm proud of you," said the puppy.
"Your wagging is just as good as mine!"

Then Jonathan ran all the way home,
the happiest kitten in the world!

And there was Karen, with another bowl of milk.
"Here, Jenny and Judy and Jimmy and Jonathan!"

They all ran over and lapped up the milk very fast.

"Did you like the milk?" asked Karen.

"Purr," said Jenny.
"Purr, purr," said Judy.
"Purr, purr, purr," said Jimmy.
"Purr, purr, purr, purr, purr,"
said Jenny and Judy and Jimmy together.

Jonathan still couldn't purr,
but he did the next best thing.
WAGGITY-WAG! WAGGITY-WAG!
WAGGITY-WAGGITY-WAGGITY-WAG!

Karen and Jenny and Judy and Jimmy
looked *so* surprised!

"Dear Jonathan," said Karen.
"You can't purr,
but you're not at all rude.
You're wagging your tail
to say 'Thank you'!"

And she picked him up and hugged him.

Watercolors and colored pencils were used for the full-color artwork.
The text type is 16 point Melior.

First United States edition published 1991.
Originally published in a German language translation under the title:
Vom Katzchen, Das Nicht Schnurren Kann.
© 1988 by Ravensburger Buchverlag Otto Maier GmbH

Library of Congress Cataloging-in-Publication Data
Titus, Eve.
The kitten who couldn't purr / by Eve Titus ; pictures by Amrei
Fechner.
p.   cm.
Summary: Jonathan the kitten asks the other animals to teach him
how to purr.
ISBN 0-688-09363-9 (trade).—ISBN 0-688-09364-7 (lib. bdg.)
[1. Cats—Fiction. 2. Animal sounds—Fiction.]
I. Fechner, Amrei, ill. II. Title.
PZ7.T543Ki   1991
[E]—dc20
90-13418   CIP   AC